ISBN: 978-1-7340687-1-9 (Paperback)

Library of Congress Control Number: 2020900777

Any references to events, people, characters or places are used fictitiously. Names, characters, and places are products of the author's imagination.

First printing edition 2020.

Happiness Mountain™ books may be purchased for business or promotional use. For information on bulk purchases, please contact Happiness Mountain Sales department by email specialmarkets@happinessmountain.com

Happiness Mountain Inc.

www.happinessmountain.com

Climbing
the
Happiness Mountain

by Ethan and Amal Indi
Illustrated by Csongor Veres

Happiness Mountain, Inc.
San Francisco, USA

"Ted, look over there!" exclaimed Mia. "That's the most beautiful mountain I've ever seen."

In the distance, peeking out above the dense forest of pine trees, was a majestic, snow-capped mountain.

"Wow! You're right, Mia. It's amazing. I want to climb it!" said Ted.

"I don't see any reason why we can't," said Mia. "I think I'm up to it! You've taught me great rock-climbing skills, big brother."

"Okay, it's settled then. We'll make camp soon and tomorrow we'll start the climb," said Ted. He was excited to get to the top.

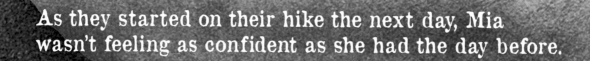

As they started on their hike the next day, Mia wasn't feeling as confident as she had the day before.

On the trail, they met up with an odd-looking, pink and polka-dotted bug. He was mumbling to himself.

"What's the matter?" asked Ted. "Are you okay?"

"No, I'm not okay. I'm not okay at all. I feel so low and sad," said the bug.

"That's how I feel today too. You must be the Low Self-Esteem Bug," said Mia. "But I know how to fix low self-esteem. I say to myself, *I am brave and strong* three times every day. I write it down in a journal and checkmark it off when I do it. It works!"

"I can do that! That's easy!" exclaimed the Low Self-Esteem Bug. He was already starting to feel better. "Do you do anything else?"

"Yes! I find something fun to do. Then, I go and do it," said Mia. "Today, we're going to climb a mountain. Do you want to come along?"

I am brave and strong
I am brave and strong
I am brave and strong

"I don't think I could do that," said the Low Self-Esteem Bug.

"Sure you can!" said Ted. "Remember to say something positive to yourself. Say I am brave and strong. When you say something positive to yourself that's true, it's called an affirmation."

"Okay, I'll try," said the bug. But, he didn't sound too confident.

"Imagine yourself climbing the mountain and reaching the top!" exclaimed Mia.

The Low Self-Esteem Bug walked with Ted and Mia.
As he walked, he pictured himself getting to the top
of the mountain with them.

When the three of them turned the bend on the trail,
they saw a red bug with horns. He was screaming
and crying at the top of his lungs.

"What's the matter?" Mia asked the bug.

"Somebody took all of my gear and now I can't climb up the mountain!" screamed the bug. He was showing his anger and getting redder and redder in the face every second.

"That's too bad," said Ted. "We have extra supplies. You can come with us."

"Why should I come with you?" asked the Anger Bug as he stomped his feet. "You probably stole my supplies and that's why you have extra!"

"That's a mean thing to say and it isn't true," said Mia. "You're just saying that because you're angry."

"I feel like my head is going to explode!" exclaimed the Anger Bug.

"That's not good," said Ted. "You can change your anger into calm if you want to."

"I've never done that before. How can I do that?" asked the Anger Bug. He was beginning to calm down.

"Just say to yourself, *I am calm and relaxed*," said Ted. "Say it three times a day, write it down in a journal, and checkmark it. If you follow those steps, you'll rarely get angry."

I am calm and relaxed
I am calm and relaxed
I am calm and relaxed

"That sounds pretty easy," said the Anger Bug. "Maybe I could come along with all of you after all."

"There's something else I do when I get angry," said Mia. "I close my eyes and take long, slow breaths three times. I try to do it every day. Why don't you try it right now?"

The Anger Bug stopped and took three long, slow breaths. When he finished, he said, "I feel so much better!"

The next morning when they woke up, Ted felt sluggish. "Come on, Ted," said Mia. It's time to get going. We'll never reach the top of the mountain if we don't make progress every day. I think the Procrastination Bug must have bitten you last night."

"Okay," said Ted. But he was moving slower than a snail. He kept wasting time and delaying their start. He didn't seem to be excited to begin the day. Finally, Mia persuaded him to get going. The four of them finally reached the base of the mountain, but Ted was out of energy. Sure enough, when they turned the corner, there was the Procrastination Bug.

"Who are you?" asked Mia. She was pretty sure she already knew, but she thought she would ask.

"I'm the Procrastination Bug, except today I got up early and did all my tasks ahead of time. I've been so helpful that everyone wants me as their mountain guide. I've never felt so energetic," said the bug.

"Uh oh, I thought so! You must have bitten my brother Ted, because he's been procrastinating all day. You must have given your procrastination to him!" said Mia.

"Oh, no! I'm so sorry. I didn't mean to give Ted my procrastination!" exclaimed the bug. "What can we do about it?"

"Well, our parents told us that when we're procrastinating, we should say, *I am helpful and I keep up with everything I need to do.* I think if Ted starts now and says it every day, then he won't procrastinate any more on this trip," said Mia.

"Maybe that would help me too," said the Procrastination Bug. "It would be great if I didn't have to procrastinate anymore."

"She helped the Low Self-Esteem Bug become confident and she helped me get rid of my anger," said the Anger Bug.

"When you feel like putting things off, just think about how happy and proud your loved ones will be when you finish the goals you've chosen," said Mia.

I am helpful and I keep up with everything I need to do.

I am helpful and I keep up with everything I need to do.

I am helpful and I keep up with everything I need to do.

Once Ted got his energy back, all five of them began to climb up the mountain. Soon, they reached a forested area with a tiny cabin. As they approached the cabin, they heard a loud voice.

"Stop! Who goes there?" the voice asked.

"We're hiking up the mountain. We thought we would stop by and say hello," said Mia.

"Do I know you?" the voice asked.

"No," said Ted. "But, we won't come closer if you don't want us to."

"You might hurt me," the voice said. "Go away."

"We're just friendly travelers," said the Anger Bug. "We don't wish harm to anyone!"

For a few minutes, the group just stood there quietly. They were about to turn and walk away when the door of the cabin opened. A blue bug with darting eyes came out. She walked toward them slowly. She had a frown on her face, until she saw the Low Self-Esteem Bug. Then, her frown began to change.

"That's my friend, the Suspicion Bug!" said the Low Self-Esteem Bug to the group. "I didn't know she lived here."

Now that she recognized her friend, the Suspicion Bug wasn't afraid anymore. She walked up to the group. "I'm sorry. I'm always afraid that someone is going to do something bad and harm me," she said. "I live here with my sister, the Worry Bug. Once she sees me talking to you, she'll probably come outdoors."

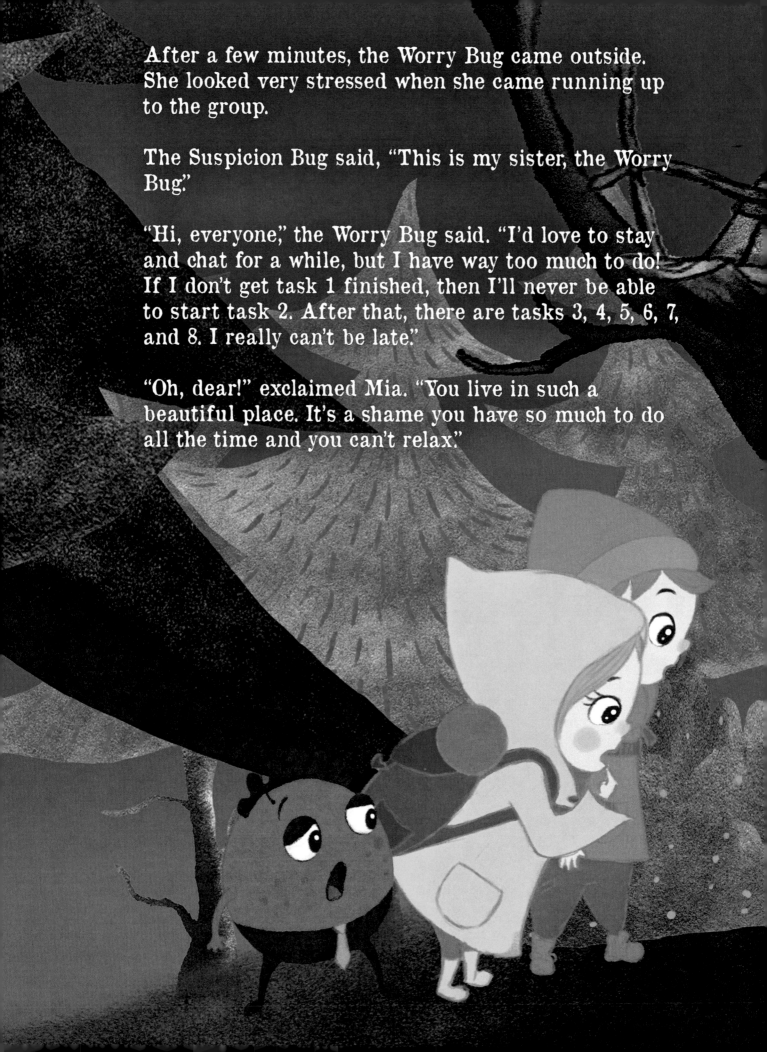

After a few minutes, the Worry Bug came outside. She looked very stressed when she came running up to the group.

The Suspicion Bug said, "This is my sister, the Worry Bug."

"Hi, everyone," the Worry Bug said. "I'd love to stay and chat for a while, but I have way too much to do! If I don't get task 1 finished, then I'll never be able to start task 2. After that, there are tasks 3, 4, 5, 6, 7, and 8. I really can't be late."

"Oh, dear!" exclaimed Mia. "You live in such a beautiful place. It's a shame you have so much to do all the time and you can't relax."

"You know, the two of you should let Mia help you. She cured me of my low self-esteem and she cured the Anger Bug and the Procrastination Bug too," said the Low Self-Esteem bug.

"I didn't cure you! You cured yourselves," said Mia. "We should all help ourselves to have happy lives. For suspicion, you can say *I am thinking positive thoughts* three times a day, write it down in a journal, and checkmark it. For worry, you can say *everything's okay* three times a day, write it down in a journal, and checkmark it."

I am thinking positive thoughts
I am thinking positive thoughts
I am thinking positive thoughts

"We can do that!" the Suspicion Bug said.

"What else can we do?" asked the Worry Bug.

"Well," said Ted, "for suspicion, you can write down three creative, positive thoughts that you have. For worry, you can stop what you're doing and take a nature walk. You can observe the beauty in nature and then write down three things that you saw."

"But, how will I have time to do that?" asked the Worry Bug. "If I do that I'll never get my work done."

"Sometimes if you take a short break, your work will get done even faster," said Mia.

Everything's okay
Everything's okay
Everything's okay

"Thanks for helping us!" said the Suspicion Bug.

"We'll take your advice! Thank you!" said the Worry Bug.

The travelers waved goodbye and continued on the trail up the mountain.

They were at the halfway point and could see that it would take a few more days to reach the top.

"We're going to make it!" Ted exclaimed. "We're getting closer now."

They were just about to make another turn in the trail when they came across two brothers, the Judgmental Bug and the Obsession Bug. They were arguing with each other.

"I'm much better than you are at climbing," said the Judgmental Bug.

"That's a mean thing to say," said the Obsession Bug. "You're getting me upset and now I need to eat and eat and eat all the honey in my honey jar."

"Uh oh," said the Anger Bug. "If they don't stop arguing they're going to get angry next."

"Or sick from too much honey!" cried Ted.

They worked together to pull the two brothers apart. Then, they showed the Judgmental Bug that he shouldn't compare himself to anyone else.

Mia said, "Everyone's different and has different talents. Sometimes you'll be better at a skill than someone else and sometimes others will have more skill than you. Instead of comparing, you should work at caring. Say to yourself, *I care about my uniqueness and I care about the feelings of others.* Write it down in your journal and checkmark it three times every day. You can also list three qualities you like about yourself and three qualities you like about your best friend."

"That's easy," said the Judgmental Bug. "My brother is my best friend."

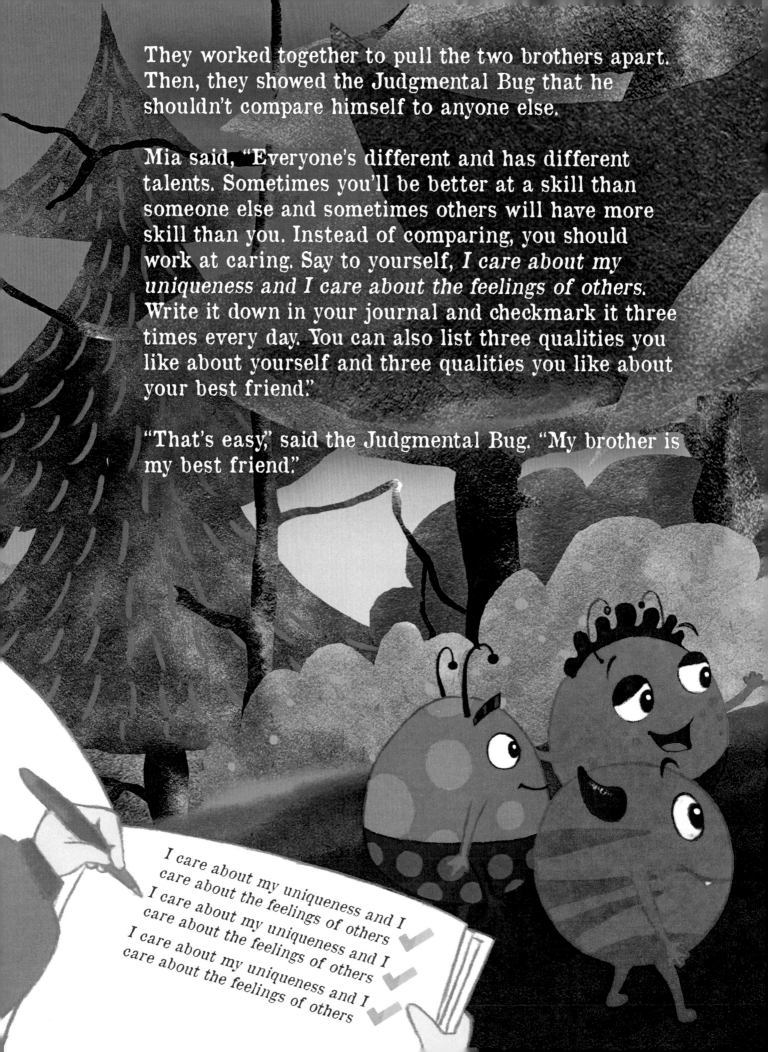

I care about my uniqueness and I care about the feelings of others
I care about my uniqueness and I care about the feelings of others
I care about my uniqueness and I care about the feelings of others

"That makes me feel good," said the Obsession Bug. "It's easier for me to control my obsessions when I feel good."

Ted said, "Yes, that's true. Every day say to yourself, *I am enough and I have enough.* Write it down in your journal and checkmark it three times. Another thing you can do is write down three things that you are grateful for. That will make you feel full of blessings."

"Thanks," said the Judgmental Bug. "I don't think we'll argue ever again."

The group waved goodbye to the two brothers and began the final ascent to the top of the mountain. When they got to the top, there was an amazing view of the surrounding countryside. It was breathtaking.

"Wow! I never thought I could do this," said the Low Self-Esteem Bug. "I'm so excited that we all made it to the top of Happiness Mountain!

"What's that over there?" asked the Anger Bug. He hadn't been angry for days.

"I don't know," said the Procrastination Bug. "What are we standing around for? Let's go check it out."

Ted and Mia smiled at each other as the group walked over to see seven huge stone monuments arranged in a circle. In the middle, there was an even larger stone, which read: *"Welcome to the top of Happiness Mountain! Few people and even fewer bugs make it here. You have conquered your negative energy. Now you can add positive energy to give yourself an even happier life! You are awesome! No one has your face, your voice, your personality, or your talents. You are unique and can be happy in your own way."*

The stone monuments each had words engraved on them. The words were acceptance, forgiveness, patience, courage, gratefulness, authenticity, and love. They read them out loud.

Mia read, "Acceptance means supporting others to reach their goals and not judging them, their skills, or their work. It also means accepting yourself."

Ted read, "Forgiveness means letting it go when someone does something that hurts you. Forgive others for making mistakes and forgive yourself too."

The Anger Bug read, "Patience means waiting for things to happen in their own time instead of whining, complaining, or getting angry. Sometimes good things take time."

The Low Self-Esteem Bug read, "Courage means being brave even if you feel a little scared. See yourself doing things with confidence and it will come true."

The Procrastination Bug read, "Gratefulness means we should recognize the blessings all around us. Our lives are filled with good and beautiful things. If we concentrate on them, we'll become more and more aware of them."

Mia and Ted teamed up to read, "Authenticity means being free to be yourself and trusting your own feelings. It also means doing the things that you believe in your heart you should do."

When they came to the last stone monument, they all read it together: "Love means being kind to everyone we meet. The more love we can give to others, the more we can feel it in our own hearts."

The group was quiet for a few minutes. Then, the Low Self-Esteem Bug said, "Let's go get the Suspicion Bug, the Worry Bug, the Judgmental Bug, and the Obsession Bug so they can see these monuments too!"

"That's a great idea! Let's go do it right now," said the Procrastination Bug.

Inspired by all they had learned on their journey, they took one last look at the beautiful view and headed down the mountain.

ANGER BUG

- [ ] I am calm and relaxed
- [ ] I am calm and relaxed
- [ ] I am calm and relaxed

LOW SELF-ESTEEM BUG

- [ ] I am brave and strong
- [ ] I am brave and strong
- [ ] I am brave and strong

PROCRASTINATION BUG

- [ ] I am helpful and I keep up with everything I need to do
- [ ] I am helpful and I keep up with everything I need to do
- [ ] I am helpful and I keep up with everything I need to do

SUSPICION BUG

- [ ] I am thinking positive thoughts
- [ ] I am thinking positive thoughts
- [ ] I am thinking positive thoughts

WORRY BUG

- [ ] Everything's okay
- [ ] Everything's okay
- [ ] Everything's okay

JUDGMENTAL BUG

- [ ] I care about my uniqueness and I care about the feelings of others
- [ ] I care about my uniqueness and I care about the feelings of others
- [ ] I care about my uniqueness and I care about the feelings of others

OBSESSION BUG

- [ ] I am enough and I have enough
- [ ] I am enough and I have enough
- [ ] I am enough and I have enough

About Authors

Amal Indi

Amal Indi is the author of The Happiness Mountain book and founder and CEO of Happiness Mountain™ Inc., a new technologically inspired wellness company. Amal believes that encouraging kids to learn the importance of positive thinking from their childhood helps them to have a happy and inspiring life. He always encourages his sons, Tehan and Ethan, to learn the importance of positive thinking.

Ethan Indi

Ethan is Amal's son. Ethan was 10 years old when he wrote this book and he goes to Brentwood Park Elementary school in Burnaby, Canada. Ethan is working on a game for kids on how to create positivity and defeat the evil thought bugs. Find out more on the www.happinessmountain.com/kids.

Amal and Ethan decided to share this story to explain negative Thought Bugs® and positive thoughts in a simple and fun way with other children.

Connect with the Authors:
amal@happinessmountain.com
ethan@happinessmountain.com
www.happinessmountain.com/kids

Made in United States
North Haven, CT
03 August 2022

22231301R00022